# Snow White
## — AND THE —
# Seven Dwarfs

A PARRAGON BOOK

Published by
Parragon Books,
Unit 13–17, Avonbridge Trading Estate,
Atlantic Road, Avonmouth, Bristol BS11 9QD

Produced by
The Templar Company plc,
Pippbrook Mill, London Road, Dorking, Surrey RH4 1JE

Designed by Mark Kingsley-Monks

Printed and bound in Italy

ISBN 0-75250-773-7

# Snow White
## — AND THE —
# Seven Dwarfs

Retold by Caroline Repchuk
Illustrated by Brian Robertson

‖ •PARRAGON• ‖

Once upon a time, as a Queen sat sewing by her window, she pricked her finger, and a drop of blood fell on the snow outside. "Oh," she sighed, "how I would love to have a child with skin as white as snow, lips as red as blood and hair as black as ebony."

A short time later her wish was granted and she had a daughter. She named her Snow White. But sadly the Queen died soon after, and the King married again. The new Queen was very beautiful, but also very cruel. She had a magic mirror and every day she asked it who was the fairest person in the land, and it would always reply truthfully that it was she.

The years passed and Snow White grew up into a beautiful young lady. So beautiful in fact that one day the Queen's mirror told her:

*"You are fair, O Queen, 'tis true,*
*But Snow White is fairer far*
*than you."*

The Queen flew into a jealous rage at the sound of the mirror's words, and from then on she was determined to get rid of Snow White, come what may.

One day a huntsman came to the palace and the evil Queen saw her chance. She told the huntsman to take Snow White into the forest and kill her. But luckily he was a kind man who took pity on Snow White and, instead of killing her, he simply left her in the woods and lied to the Queen on his return.

Snow White was very afraid, for it was dark among the trees and full of strange noises. She walked deeper and deeper into the forest until at last she came upon a little house.

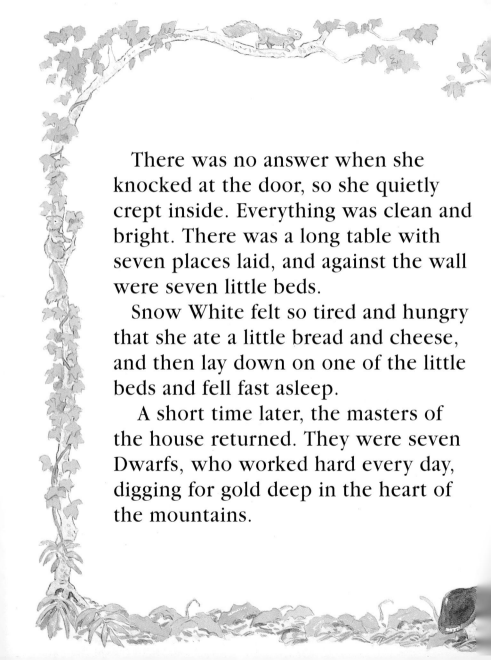

There was no answer when she knocked at the door, so she quietly crept inside. Everything was clean and bright. There was a long table with seven places laid, and against the wall were seven little beds.

Snow White felt so tired and hungry that she ate a little bread and cheese, and then lay down on one of the little beds and fell fast asleep.

A short time later, the masters of the house returned. They were seven Dwarfs, who worked hard every day, digging for gold deep in the heart of the mountains.

The Dwarfs saw at once that someone had been eating at their table, and were quite alarmed until one of them spotted Snow White still curled up fast asleep

on one of their little beds. As soon as they looked at her, they were enchanted by her beauty and decided to let her sleep on until morning.

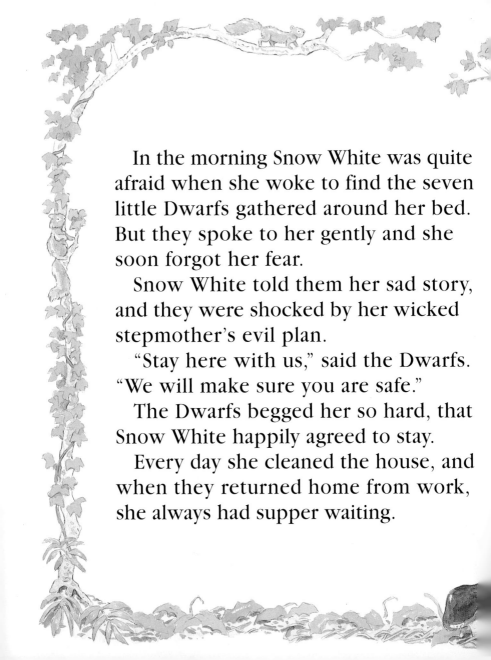

In the morning Snow White was quite afraid when she woke to find the seven little Dwarfs gathered around her bed. But they spoke to her gently and she soon forgot her fear.

Snow White told them her sad story, and they were shocked by her wicked stepmother's evil plan.

"Stay here with us," said the Dwarfs. "We will make sure you are safe."

The Dwarfs begged her so hard, that Snow White happily agreed to stay.

Every day she cleaned the house, and when they returned home from work, she always had supper waiting.

Meanwhile, back at the castle, the Queen was happy to be rid of Snow White, and to be the most beautiful woman in the land once more. But one day she asked her mirror:

*"Mirror, mirror, on the wall,*
*Who is the fairest of us all?"*

And the mirror replied:

*"You are fair, O Queen, 'tis true,*
*But Snow White is fairer far*
*than you.*
*Snow White, who dwells with the*
*seven small men,*
*Is as fair as you and as fair again."*

The Queen was horrified when she heard this, and realised that the huntsman had deceived her.

For days the Queen thought of ways to be rid of her rival, and at last she made a plan. She disguised herself as an old tinker woman in a shabby bonnet and shawl and, leaning heavily on an old stick, she hobbled off into the forest. No one would recognise her as the evil Queen!

Finally she came to the house of the seven Dwarfs and called at the door:

"Fine wares to sell!"

Snow White peeked shyly out of the window and smiled at her.

The old woman held up some laces made of pretty coloured silk.

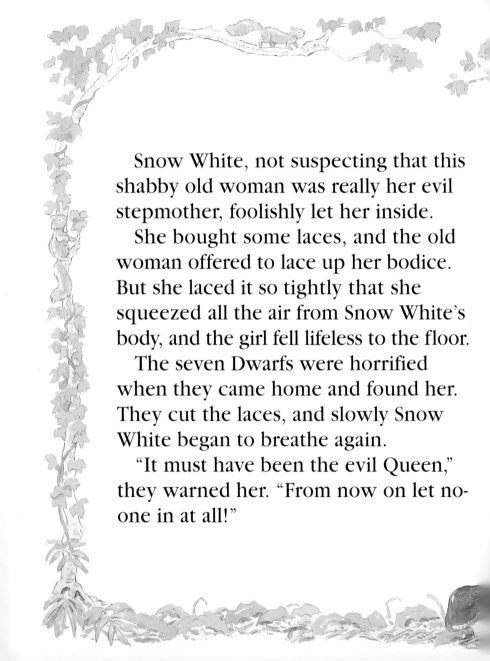

Snow White, not suspecting that this shabby old woman was really her evil stepmother, foolishly let her inside.

She bought some laces, and the old woman offered to lace up her bodice. But she laced it so tightly that she squeezed all the air from Snow White's body, and the girl fell lifeless to the floor.

The seven Dwarfs were horrified when they came home and found her. They cut the laces, and slowly Snow White began to breathe again.

"It must have been the evil Queen," they warned her. "From now on let no-one in at all!"

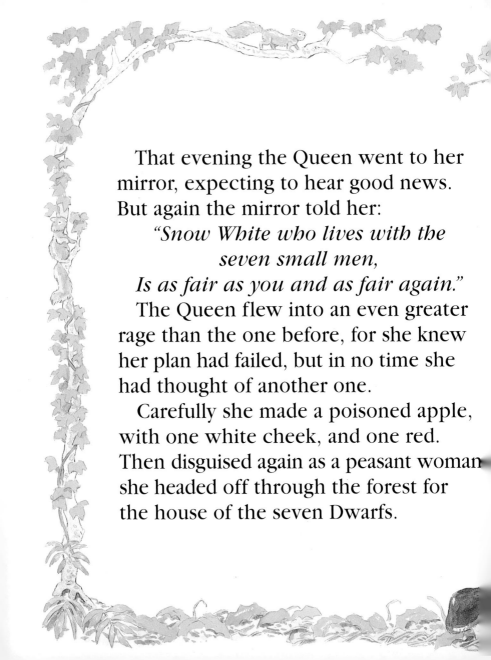

That evening the Queen went to her mirror, expecting to hear good news. But again the mirror told her:

*"Snow White who lives with the seven small men,*
*Is as fair as you and as fair again."*

The Queen flew into an even greater rage than the one before, for she knew her plan had failed, but in no time she had thought of another one.

Carefully she made a poisoned apple, with one white cheek, and one red. Then disguised again as a peasant woman she headed off through the forest for the house of the seven Dwarfs.

When she arrived, she knocked at
the door and invited Snow White
to taste the beautiful apple.

Snow White remembered what the Dwarfs had said and would not let her in. But the old woman cut the apple in half and began to eat the white half.

"This is delicious," she said. And poor Snow White thought that, as the woman was eating it, it could do her no harm. She did not realise that only the red half was poisoned.

So Snow White stretched out her hand for the red half and took a bite. In an instant she fell down dead on the ground.

The evil Queen cackled with delight. And that evening her mirror told her:

*"You are most fair, my Lady Queen,
No fairer face is to be seen."*

When the Dwarfs returned home
from work they wept to find Snow
White lying dead upon the ground.
They searched the house, but could
not discover what had
happened to her.

They could not bring themselves to bury their beautiful Snow White in the hard ground, so they put her in a glass coffin and placed it on the hill behind their house. Sadly, they took turns to watch over her.

Days passed, and still Snow
White looked as lovely as ever.
She looked just as if she were
in a deep sleep.

Then one day a Prince came riding through the forest. When he saw Snow White he fell immediately in love with her beautiful face. The Dwarfs took pity on him, and decided to let him take her coffin to his castle.

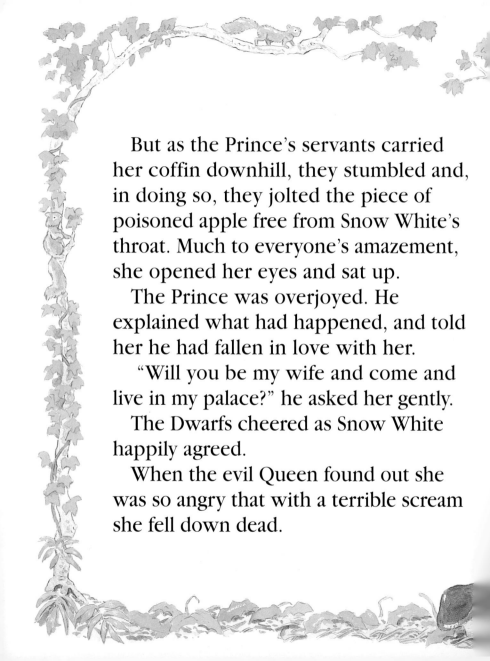

But as the Prince's servants carried her coffin downhill, they stumbled and, in doing so, they jolted the piece of poisoned apple free from Snow White's throat. Much to everyone's amazement, she opened her eyes and sat up.

The Prince was overjoyed. He explained what had happened, and told her he had fallen in love with her.

"Will you be my wife and come and live in my palace?" he asked her gently.

The Dwarfs cheered as Snow White happily agreed.

When the evil Queen found out she was so angry that with a terrible scream she fell down dead.

And so Snow White and the Prince were married, and as with all good fairy tales, they lived happily ever after.

## Jacob and Wilhelm Grimm

The German Brothers Grimm, Jacob
(1785-1863) and Wilhelm (1786-1859) gathered
together over 200 old folk tales to form the
classic collection of stories now known as
*Grimm's Fairy Tales*.
Before this time, *Snow White and the
Seven Dwarfs* and the other tales would have
been part of an oral tradition of storytelling.
Retold from generation to generation, they
passed on important truths about everyday life
and our fellow creatures: good would be
rewarded and evil would not go unpunished.
A child's hidden anxieties were given shape in
the form of witches and ogres and they saw that
time and again, the underdog would emerge
victor. These simple messages remain a valuable
contribution to each child's development of
a sense of "right" and "wrong" and help explain
why *Grimm's Fairy Tales* are so well-loved
throughout the world.